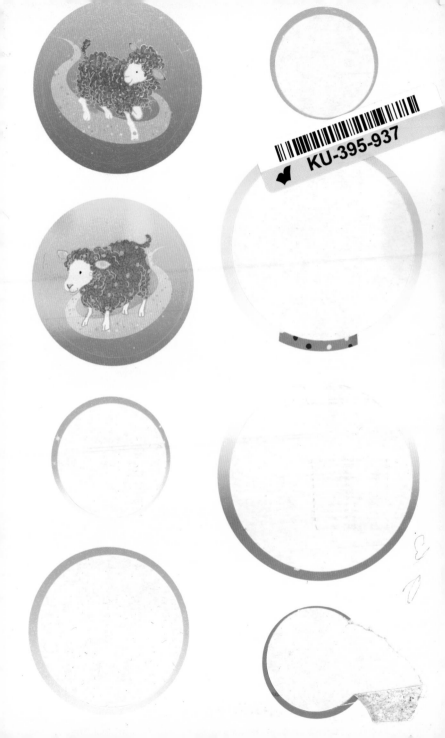

Magic Farm

A Whole New World

Ashley Birch

EGMONT

Books in the Magic Farm series

A Whole New World

A Big Surprise!

This book belongs to:

....

With special thanks to Valerie Wilding
For Stanley and Molly

EGMONT

We bring stories to life

Magic Farm: A Whole New World
First published in Great Britain 2011
by Egmont UK Limited
239 Kensington High Street
London W8 6SA

ISBN 978 1 4052 5134 1

1 3 5 7 9 10 8 6 4 2

www.egmont.co.uk

A CIP catalogue record for this title is available from the British Library

Printed and bound in Great Britain by CPI

CONTENTS

Mystery in the Mist

Olly tried not to giggle as his sister,

Hannah, clambered down the steps

of the chicken coop. She had fluffy

feathers stuck all over her chin, and

straw in her hair!

'No eggs again?' Olly asked.

'Not one,' Hannah replied.

'Egg-straordinary!' said Olly.

'Ha ha.' Hannah blew the feathers off her chin. 'Olly, why won't our hens lay us any eggs? We must be doing something wrong. But what?'

'I don't know,' he said. 'But we need to find out soon!'

3

They walked across the yard to the farmhouse. Hannah hung the empty egg bowl on its hook by the door. 'I've mucked out Ebony's stable and she's out grazing. I'll find her a nice juicy carrot. Have you finished your chores?'

Olly showed her his filthy hands. 'I've watered the vegetable patch, and there's not a weed in sight.' He looked around. 'Doesn't it all look great?'

The Thompson family had only lived at Golden Valley Farm for a few weeks. It had been overgrown and run down when they moved in, but Hannah, Olly and their mum and dad had worked hard. It was beginning to look like a real farm. Spring had begun, so crops and vegetables were showing their first green leaves, there was a horse in the stable, and the sheep were due to arrive soon. The only problem was the chickens. They refused to lay eggs.

'What are you looking at?' Hannah asked Olly.

Olly was gazing at the hill behind

the farm. 'The trees there are huge. I bet I could find some great leaves for my collection.'

Hannah rolled her eyes. 'Haven't you got enough already? Oh, come on, then. We'll get a great view across Golden Valley from up there.'

A few minutes later they made it to the top of the hill, both puffed out.

'Aidan!' Olly shouted, breaking into a big grin.

Their neighbour Aidan was sitting on a tree branch, nibbling the last bits of an apple core. 'Hi!' he said. 'You two looked as if you were struggling to make it all the way up here.'

'*Hannah* was struggling,' said Olly.

'I was just waiting for her.'

His sister poked him. 'I'm faster than you any day!'

'I'm faster than both of you,' said

Aidan, swinging his long legs back and forth.

Olly looked down the grassy slope on the opposite side of the hill from Golden Valley Farm. Mist swirled below, hiding the bottom of the hill. About halfway down stood a large scarecrow, one arm outstretched.

'See that?' Olly said. 'Let's race.

Last one to get there's a –'

He yelped as Aidan's apple core bounced off his head. Then Aidan jumped from the tree branch and landed beside him.

'Go!' shrieked Hannah.

They streaked away. Aidan was soon in the lead, running so fast his legs were almost a blur. Hannah was next, but Olly was catching up. He wasn't going to let Hannah beat him! He grabbed at her sleeve, trying to pull her back, but instead he toppled forwards.

'Whooooooaah!' he yelled as he tumbled down, down, down, pulling Hannah with him. They rolled over and over, laughing.

Aidan's voice floated up the hill. 'I wiiiiin!' Olly and Hannah sat up, and watched him run.

'Uh oh . . . He's going too fast to stop,' said Hannah.

'Heeelp!' wailed Aidan. He grabbed the scarecrow's outstretched arm and whirled round. The scarecrow span round, too.

The sound of Aidan's voice faded away. Everything went quiet. Olly clutched at Hannah's arm. 'Where's Aidan gone?'

Hannah gulped. 'He's . . . vanished.'

Chasing Chickens

Olly leapt up, and ran down to look at the scarecrow. 'It *seems* normal,' he said, as Hannah reached his side. Then his eyes lit up. 'Hey! Just before Aidan disappeared, he grabbed the scarecrow's arm and span it round. Right? I wonder . . .'

Before he could finish, Hannah took a deep breath, grasped the stuffed arm and walked in a circle. She moved slowly at first, then faster, her hair fanning out behind her in the sunlight. Then . . .

Olly gasped. Hannah was gone!

What on earth was going on?

There's only one way to find out, he thought. He took hold of the scarecrow's arm and walked round. The scarecrow turned with him . . . faster . . . faster. Olly felt a tingling in his body.

'Huh?'

The mist had cleared. Below, in

a deep valley of shimmering grass,
nestled a pretty farmhouse. Scarlet
creeper climbed the honey-coloured
walls, and a white picket fence
surrounded the yard. Beyond, was

a vegetable garden, an orchard and small fields.

'What . . . where . . .?' Olly said. He turned and found his sister and Aidan, looking as surprised as he was.

Aidan shook his head, confused. 'I've never seen this farm before. We just . . . I dunno.'

Behind them, instead of the steep hill, was a thick forest.

Hannah looked up. 'That's odd.' Puffy clouds bobbed in the sky, but they weren't white: some were palest pink, others were blue or gold. And the sun was different. You could look at it without squinting your eyes. 'It's sparkling,' Hannah whispered, 'like a diamond. And it's shooting out rainbow sparks.'

The boys spotted a huge purple machine parked beside a barn.

'It's a combine harvester,' said Olly.

'It's a tractor,' said Aidan.

'Rubbish!' argued Hannah. 'It's a steam engine – look, it has a chimney. But why is there a big whistle on the front of it?'

Olly set off towards the farmhouse. 'Let's take a look.'

As they neared the fence, Olly noticed people in the farmyard and vegetable garden. 'They're not doing much,' he said, curious. 'In fact, none of them seem to be moving at all.'

One figure was frozen in the act of reaching for a wheelbarrow. Two more looked as if they were about to dig up potatoes. They were as still as statues.

But something else *was* moving. Chickens! They clucked, squawked and scurried all around. There were chickens with blue feathers in the vegetable garden, green chickens in the farmyard. There was even a big chicken with purple feathers sprouting out of its head, just like a crown!

'I've never seen chickens like these before,' Hannah said, gazing around.

'Look,' said Aidan. 'The fencing that goes round their coop isn't fastened properly – the wire netting is loose, and they've escaped. If they run off they'll be in danger from foxes.'

'Let's try to round them all up,' said Hannah.

'Wait,' said Olly. 'We better ask before we go in the

farmyard. Hey! Excuse me!' he yelled at the quiet workers.

None of them moved.

'Want help with these chickens?' shouted Aidan.

Still nothing. Olly looked at them more closely. Their clothes were ragged. And was that straw under their hats? He peered at the nearest worker's face.

'No *way*! Their faces are stitched on,' exclaimed Olly. 'They're not real people – they're scarecrows!'

The others stared. 'You're right,' said Hannah. 'Someone's propped them up to look like farm workers. Maybe it's a countryside museum.'

'But it *must* be a real farm, with all these chickens running about,' Aidan pointed out.

Three tiny chicks scuttled through the fence. Olly scooped one up. Hannah gently caught the next and Aidan chased and caught the third.

Hannah smoothed her chick's pink fluff. 'Aaah, cute!'

'They should be in the coop,' said Olly. 'Come on. Let's go and find the farmer.' He climbed the fence, then turned to help Hannah over.

She brushed him off. 'I can do it!'

Olly laughed. 'So can Aidan. Look!'

Aidan had given Hannah his chick, then backed away, so he could take a run at the fence. He sped towards it, leapt into the air and sailed over.

Olly led Hannah and Aidan past the scarecrow by the wheelbarrow. Suddenly, he heard a muffled sound. *Ha-hat-tishoo!* He nearly jumped out of his skin!

Aidan prodded him in the back. 'Get a move on, slow coach!'

'Didn't you hear that?'

'What?' said Aidan.

'The scarecrow,' said Olly, his eyes widening.

'What about it?' asked Hannah.

Olly swallowed. 'It sneezed.'

The Hayseeds

'Sneezing scarecrows – yeah, right!'

'Aidan, it did!' said Olly. 'You heard it, Hannah, didn't you?'

But Hannah was heading for the farmhouse. 'Come *on* guys. Hurry up!'

She brushed against a scarecrow in a floppy blue patchwork hat.

It jumped out of her way!

All three friends stopped.

'It moved!' whispered Olly. 'Didn't it?'

Hannah nodded. 'I think so.'

'It couldn't have,' said Aidan.

The farm was silent except for the

steady *cheep, cheep* from the chicks.

Aidan poked the scarecrow.

'Ooooh! Don't hurt me!' it squealed from between neatly stitched lips.

Hannah gasped. 'Did you speak?' she whispered to the scarecrow in amazement. It looked scared. 'We won't hurt you,' Hannah added.

The scarecrow trembled. 'Well . . .

you don't look like Little Rotters.

Are you . . . are you Big Rotters?'

Its forehead wrinkled.

'No!' said Olly. 'We're just children.

What on earth are Rotters?'

'Don't be afraid. We're very nice

children,' continued Hannah. 'We

want to help. Look.' She showed the

scarecrows the two chicks cradled in

her hands. 'We stopped the chicks from getting into danger.'

The scarecrow smiled slowly. 'Oh, thank you. You can't be Rotters, then. A Little Rotter wouldn't be kind like that.' He bent stiffly to pick a blade of grass. Then he clasped his hands with the grass between his thumbs, put it to his mouth and blew.

Eeeeeee! A shrill whistling sound screeched out from the grass.

More scarecrows hurried towards them.

'These are all my friends,' said the first scarecrow. 'I'm Patch, and we're the Hayseeds. We look after this farm.'

'But who does the farm belong to?' asked Aidan.

The scarecrows glanced at each

other, and then down at the ground. If their cheeks hadn't been made of cloth, Olly was certain they would have been blushing bright red. Were they embarrassed?

'Well, erm . . .' began one.

'The thing is . . .' started another.

The one called Patch folded his arms. 'The thing is, we don't know.

All we *do* know is that we woke up here one day and the farmhouse was empty. We're trying to keep things running until the farmer comes back.'

'*If* he comes back,' said one of the scarecrows, shaking his head.

'We have a spot of trouble now and then,' said a particularly scruffy

44

scarecrow, 'but we do our very best.'
He pointed to a cheery scarecrow in
a yellow hat. 'She is Sunny Hayseed,'
he told them, 'and I'm called Muck.'

'*Ha-hat-tishoo!*' sneezed another,
and his hat blew off.

'That's Tishoo,' said Patch. 'You'll
remember *his* name! We're happy to
meet you. Welcome to Magic Farm!'

Patch started walking. 'Follow me, please,' he called. As he strode off, he tore his sleeve on a prickly bush.

'Oh dear, oh dear,' he muttered. 'That means another patch.'

'Don't worry,' said Sunny, smiling. 'We'll mend you.'

'Hey, now we know how Patch got *his* name,' Olly whispered to Hannah and Aidan, with a grin.

Soon the children and scarecrows were all settled on hay bales in the sparkling sunshine. A purple chicken skittered between Aidan's long legs, squawking at being disturbed. Muck scooped it up and took it back to the chicken coop. He placed the chicken inside, then leant a flower pot against the wire netting that had come loose.

'That'll do for now,' Muck muttered, 'but we'll need to fix it properly soon. They could still get out.'

'So, what's all this trouble you're having?' asked Olly.

'It's the Little Rotters!' said Patch. 'They're so naughty. They put slimy slugs in the greenhouse that eat all the lettuce. They even put mould in our beds to make our straw rot.'

'They sneak up and pull out our stuffing,' said Sunny, with a shiver. 'Once I stood up and found I had an empty leg. Down I went!'

'You poor thing,' said Hannah.

'But what *are* the Little Rotters?' asked Olly.

Sunny looked over her shoulder, as if she was checking whether any one was listening. Then she leant in very close to Olly and the others.

'If you see small people with tufts of orange hair, hiding behind things and laughing nastily, they're Little Rotters.'

Olly frowned. 'Why do they want to cause trouble?'

Sunny shrugged and gave a big sigh. 'Who knows? They just love it.'

'It was the Little Rotters who

broke the chicken coop,' said Muck, as he settled on a hay bale. 'Now all the chickens are running about in a flap.'

'We haven't done any of our chores this morning,' said Sunny. 'No one's juiced the cows and there's been no time to curl the pigs' tails. We've been too busy chasing chickens.'

'Curl the pigs' tails!' Hannah repeated, laughing. 'Don't they just curl by themselves?'

Sunny and Muck shared a look, as if they thought Hannah was crazy.

'Oh no. Someone has to curl them every morning,' Muck explained.

Olly jumped up. 'We'll help you,'

he said. 'Let's pop these chicks in the wheelbarrow so they can't run away again. Now for those big chickens.'

They followed Tishoo over to the strawberry patch. 'There's one . . . *Ha-hat-tishoo!*' The scarecrow's hat blew off and landed over a chicken. Aidan easily caught that one. Next they went with Muck to the cow field, where they chased a red chicken and Muck slipped in a great big, sloppy cowpat. Olly helped him up while Hannah coaxed the chicken towards her.

'You're filthy, Muck,' said Olly.

'I always am,' said Muck, grinning. 'I just can't seem to help it.'

Suddenly they heard loud, frantic

squawking coming from inside the
farmhouse. They all rushed indoors
and found Sunny chasing a spotty

chicken round the kitchen table.

'Whee! Wahey!' the scarecrow cried when Olly caught the chicken under a tea towel.

Carefully, Olly carried the chicken outside. Aidan had found some bits of spare wood, and was busy mending the coop. Olly lowered the chicken back into its home and the two boys gently lifted the baby chicks from the wheelbarrow and placed them into the coop. Soon, all the chickens were safe.

'Thanks,' said Patch. 'You've really helped. Farming's hard work!'

'I know,' said Olly. 'We live on a farm too. The work never finishes. It's lots of fun, though. I love playing with all the animals.' He watched the colourful chickens. 'Hey, are their eggs different colours too?'

Patch nodded, bits of straw flying from beneath his hat.

'That lavender-coloured one there,' said Muck, 'she lays blue eggs. That speckled hen, she lays green ones. But lately none of them are laying *any* eggs at all. We don't know why.'

Olly frowned. 'Hmm. We've got the same problem at our farm.'

'Oh my!' Patch leapt up suddenly. 'Oh my, oh my! Someone's missing.'

'Who?' asked Olly, as Patch ran wildly in circles.

'Henrietta!' he wailed.

We Can Help!

'What does Henrietta look like?' asked Hannah.

'Her feathers have sparkly bits,' said Patch, 'and her tail is purple.'

'Is she a scarecrow?' asked Olly.

He was looking very puzzled.

'No, she's a chicken,' Sunny replied, the threads of her mouth turned down in a frown.

'We need to find her before the Little Rotters steal her!' cried Patch.

'Would they really try to take her?' Aidan asked. 'That sounds a bit much even for the Rotters!'

Patch dipped a straw hand into his jacket pocket and pulled out an egg. Olly gasped. It was silver!

'Henrietta lays these,' Patch said.

'Well, she used to. This is the only one left.' He put the egg carefully back in his pocket.

'The Little Rotters love her silver eggs because they're so shiny,' Tishoo went on. 'That's why they might steal her. *Ha-hat-tishoo!*'

'We'd better hurry up then!' said Hannah, catching Tishoo's hat as it sailed towards her like a floppy frisbee. 'Let's try the barn first. I bet it's cosy in there – maybe she likes it.'

'It is cosy,' said Tishoo. 'It's where we sleep.'

They hurried to the red-painted barn. As they stepped inside, Olly noticed a great big empty space right in the middle.

'That's where we keep the Duzzit,' Sunny said. 'Best farm machine there ever was.'

'Oh, you mean that big purple tractor-combine-engine thingie!' said Hannah. 'But why is it called the Duzzit?'

Sunny laughed. 'Because whatever we need done, it Duzzit!'

'I get it,' said Olly. 'It *does it*! Cool! Later, can we see it in action?'

'Of course! As soon as we find Henrietta.'

The search began. They looked in every corner, behind the gigantic log pile, and along shelves lined with strange, unfamiliar tools . . . but they had no luck.

Aidan climbed a ladder to the hayloft.

'That's our bedroom,' said Patch. 'We haven't made our beds today, so don't look, will you?'

Aidan laughed. 'I won't be able to see Henrietta if I don't look!' He disappeared from view.

The others watched the top of the

ladder, waiting for Aidan to reappear.

They waited. And waited.

'Something's happened,' whispered Hannah.

'Uh-oh. Little Rotters, I'll bet,' said Patch.

'BOO!'

They all whipped round. There, with his arms folded and a very big,

cheeky grin, was Aidan!

'Very funny,' Olly said. 'How did you get down from the loft without us seeing?'

Aidan showed them another ladder on the other side of the barn. 'What goes up, must come down.'

'But Henrietta wasn't up there, was she?' said Hannah. 'OK, let's try the orchard and along the hedgerows.'

They made their way to the orchard where rows and rows of fruit trees and bushes were growing.

Olly checked some low branches, heavy with fruit. 'Hey! Apples and oranges grow together on this tree!'

'Look, I've found apricot bushes,' said Aidan in surprise.

'Here's a raspberry tree!' Hannah called.

Aidan snorted. 'Don't be daft,' he said, 'raspberries don't grow on tr–'

Hannah popped a fat raspberry in his open mouth. 'They do here. Anything can happen on Magic Farm! But magic or not, we still haven't found Henrietta.'

Just beyond the amazing orchard,

Olly noticed a pond of gleaming water.

It looked like jewels were floating on

the surface and – was that a three-legged duck he could see? 'What about the pond?' he suggested. 'Who knows, chickens on this farm might swim!'

'Good idea, Olly!' said Hannah.

They ran to the pond and the duck waddled away on its three legs to hide in a thick clump of bulrushes.

Patch came lolloping over to join them. Bits of straw stuck out of a fresh tear in his sleeve. Olly poked the straw back. 'There. Can't have you getting any thinner, can we?'

Hannah frowned. 'I still don't see Henrietta anywhere,' she said, glumly. 'Where could she be?'

Suddenly, Olly spotted a cluster of

three-toed markings in the muddy edge of the pond. 'Look! Footprints.'

'F-f-footprints?' said Patch.

'Tiny ones,' said Olly.

'T-tiny f-footprints?' Patch gulped. He looked over to where Olly was pointing. 'Those aren't Henrietta's! It's the Little Rotters! *Run!*'

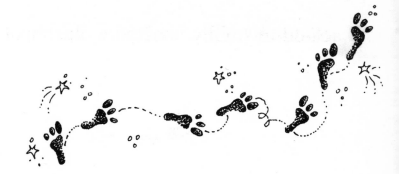

Little Rotters!

Patch and the other Hayseeds sped away. Olly and Aidan began to chase after them.

'Wait!' Hannah called, pulling them back. She held a finger to her lips.

'Ssh! I just heard something. I think something's here.' She crept towards a patch of ferns, near to the water's edge.

The ferns rustled and shook. Hannah jumped back in fright.

Out from the greenery walked . . .

. . . a plump chicken with sparkly bits and purple tail feathers!

Hannah, Olly and Aidan all laughed

out loud.

'So you must be Henrietta,' said

Hannah in delight, scooping her up.

'Let's get you back to all your chicky

friends and the Hayseeds. Olly! What are you doing?'

He was burrowing among the ferns. 'Wow!' he cried. 'You'll never guess what I've found!'

Aidan and Hannah exchanged a puzzled look.

Olly backed out and held up his trophy. 'An egg!'

'Well done, Henrietta,' said Hannah. 'A lovely silver egg.'

As they ambled to the farmyard, Olly said, 'Henrietta seems to like it better outdoors than in the chicken coop. I don't blame her. I'd rather play outside than be cooped up indoors. Hey!' He laughed. 'Cooped up . . . chicken coop . . . get it?'

The others rolled their eyes, but Olly didn't notice. He'd just spotted something very strange. A face peered out from behind a gatepost. A small face topped with a tuft of orange hair. The face grinned, then it was gone.

'Did you see that?' said Olly.

'What?' asked Aidan.

Hannah gasped. 'Look! Behind that

tree trunk. Oh, it's gone. I think it was a Little Rotter.'

'That must be what I saw, too,' said Olly.

'Come on.' Aidan found a long twig and poked among the grass and wild flowers. 'Let's find more. I want to see them properly!'

'Me, too!' said Hannah.

'We have to try to stop them causing trouble for the Hayseeds,' added Olly.

Aidan pointed his twig at a craggy rock. 'There are two of them behind there,' he whispered.

Olly froze as a pair of little faces peered round the rock. Their eyes glittered and they grinned wickedly.

'Go 'way!' said one in an odd, screechy voice.

'You stay away from the Hayseeds,' Hannah shouted.

'Oooh! Yucky yuck! We don't like children,' said the other Little Rotter. 'Go 'WAY!'

'We will, if you promise to leave the Hayseeds alone,' Aidan replied.

'Maybe we will, maybe we won't,' jeered the first Little Rotter, cackling loudly. 'You go 'way. Or else!'

Aidan and Hannah took a step backwards.

'Yikes!' said Olly. 'They're scary. Well, at least we tried. But now I think we really had better run!'

The frightened Hayseeds were waiting for them as they arrived back in the farmyard.

'You've found Henrietta!' Patch cried happily.

'We found some Little Rotters too,' gasped Olly.

'Oooh!' Patch and Muck groaned, huddling together.

'We told them to leave you alone,' said Aidan, puffing out his chest. 'I don't think they'll bother you again.'

Olly didn't think Aidan sounded very sure. 'Well, maybe not for a while,' he whispered to Hannah. He remembered the Rotters' grins.

'Henrietta's back! I'm so happy,' squealed Sunny. 'I'm going to dance!'

She hopped and skipped across the cobbles, making everyone laugh.

Muck gave Olly a high-five.

Tishoo was so excited he sneezed his hat right into the pigsty.

Olly proudly held out the silver egg. 'Look what Henrietta did!'

'Hurray! She laid an egg at last!' Sunny said excitedly.

'Let's cook it for lunch!' Patch suggested.

'You children like eggs, don't you?' asked Sunny.

Olly, Aidan and Hannah all nodded eagerly.

'I wish scarecrows could eat,' said Patch. 'I tried potatoes once, but the lumps fell down through my straw and out the ankles of my trousers!'

They all went into the kitchen. While Sunny cooked, Olly told the scarecrows how Henrietta seemed to like finding her own nesting place, rather than being stuck in the coop. As he was explaining, he thought about the hens at Golden Valley; they hadn't been laying eggs either.

Perhaps they want to make their own nests on the farm, just like Henrietta?

The Hayseeds listened carefully to what Olly told them. 'Of course, we want our chickens to be happy,' Patch said, nodding. 'We'd like to let them run wherever they want –'

'Great!' said Hannah.

'– but we can't.'

'Why not?' asked Olly.

'Because of those Little Rotters,' Patch explained. 'We can't let them chase our chickens. There's nothing we can do.'

Those naughty little Rotters were spoiling things again.

Where's Golden Valley?

'Lunch!' Sunny called.

On the table were three enormous plates of juicy scrambled egg and hot buttered toast.

'Hey! How did you make enough

scrambled eggs for three?' Hannah asked the scarecrows.

'A silver egg always makes enough for anyone who's hungry,' said Sunny. 'Didn't you know that?'

Everybody laughed, but Olly still couldn't stop thinking about how to help the chickens. He found a pencil and paper and started doodling while he munched. 'Look!' he cried, a few minutes later. 'The chickens need somewhere to roam free, right?'

'Right,' everyone chorused.

'But they have to be safe from the Little Rotters, right?'

'Right.'

'Then we must find a lovely little bit of the farm,' said Olly, 'with bushes and ditches and other fun

hiding places where they can roost.

And I've designed a special fence.

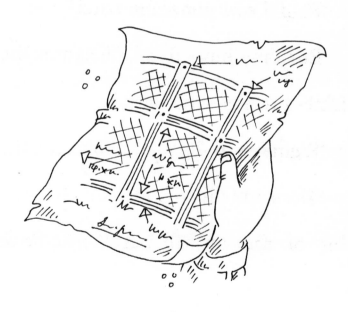

See? It's impossible for any creature – or Little Rotter – to climb over it.'

'Brilliant,' said Aidan. 'Let's get to work! I'll sort out some fence posts.'

Hannah jumped up. 'I saw some wire netting in the barn.'

'We have to dig some holes for the posts,' said Olly.

'The Duzzit will help!' cried the

scarecrows leaping in excitement.

They raced out of the kitchen towards the huge, purple machine.

Olly and Hannah climbed into the seat and turned a large green key. The Duzzit roared into life. Patch called instructions as they rode the amazing machine, which used long arms to dig holes and hammer in the posts that Aidan had collected.

'Fence-building is fun!' Hannah cried.

The Duzzit chugged and steamed along, and they took turns pulling the chain to make the whistle blow. *Wheeeeup! Wheeeeup!*

By late afternoon, when the sun's sparkle had changed from diamond

white to dusky pink, the fence was in place. Now the chickens could explore their own safe garden!

Everyone perched on the Duzzit to watch.

'They need feeding,' said Muck.

Sunny pressed a red knob on the side of the Duzzit. A flap opened, and shiny red buckets of corn popped out on a big tray. Olly, Hannah and Aidan grabbed a handle each and went to scatter handfuls of yellow corn across the ground. The chickens pecked excitedly around their feet.

As they emptied the last of the corn from the buckets, Patch came up to them. 'Here,' he said. 'Have a carrot, each of you. Muck pulled them up for you, to say thank you for all your help today.'

'Don't worry!' Muck laughed. 'I washed the muck off!'

Olly took a big bite. 'Mmm. Yum! Crunchy!'

'They're *really* sweet!' said Aidan. He was right; the carrots tasted more like ice cream than carrot.

Hannah sighed. 'I guess we should go home. Mum and Dad will worry if we're gone too long.' She gazed at the forest that surrounded Magic Farm. 'But how do we get back?'

Patch pointed. 'See that scarecrow over near the trees? The one that doesn't walk or talk? That's where I first saw you. I'll take you back.'

Sunny and Muck said goodbye. Tishoo sneezed so hard that his hat sailed over the barn.

When they reached the scarecrow, Patch said, 'Goodbye, and thank you again. You'll always be welcome at Magic Farm.'

Olly span round the scarecrow, but nothing happened. He frowned. 'Hey it's not working! Any ideas?'

'Wait!' said Aidan. 'We're going *back*, so let's spin it the other way. Here goes.' He span the scarecrow backwards, and vanished!

Hannah was next, and finally Olly. He was glad to find the others waiting for him in Golden Valley.

'I'm off home,' said Aidan, waving.

'See you next time. Let's go back to Magic Farm soon!'

Hannah and Olly watched him leave, then they hurried over the hill towards their own farm. 'Let's tell Mum and Dad how to get the chickens to lay eggs,' said Olly. 'They'll be so pleased.' He looked around and spotted a corner of the farmyard that led out to a fenced grassy field with shrubs and banks. 'That would be perfect!' he cried, pointing. He could just imagine the hens building their nests and laying eggs. They were close enough to the farmhouse to be safe, but they'd have lots of space to roam around.

'I don't think we should mention

Magic Farm to Mum and Dad,' said Hannah. 'They'd never believe us.'

Olly stopped in his tracks. 'But it *was* real, wasn't it? Or did we just imagine it?'

Hannah grinned, reaching into her pocket. She pulled out Muck's carrot. 'Look. A treat for Ebony!'

'Hooray!' said Olly. 'Magic Farm *is*

real after all. And now that we know how to get there, we can go back and see the Hayseeds anytime we like! Now life in Golden Valley is going to be even more fun!'

EGMONT PRESS: ETHICAL PUBLISHING

Egmont Press is about turning writers into successful authors and children into passionate readers – producing books that enrich and entertain. As a responsible children's publisher, we go even further, considering the world in which our consumers are growing up.

Safety First
Naturally, all of our books meet legal safety requirements. But we go further than this; every book with play value is tested to the highest standards – if it fails, it's back to the drawing-board.

Made Fairly
We are working to ensure that the workers involved in our supply chain – the people that make our books – are treated with fairness and respect.

Responsible Forestry
We are committed to ensuring all our papers come from environmentally and socially responsible forest sources.

For more information, please visit our website at
www.egmont.co.uk/ethicalpublishing

There's lots more fun to be had at **Magic Farm!**

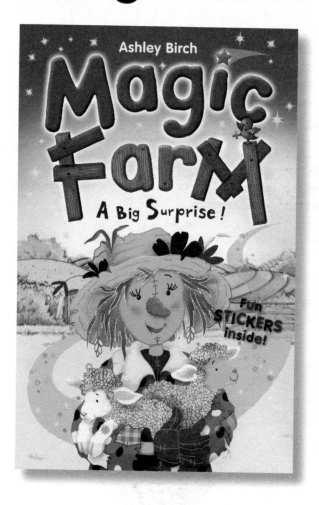